THE SECRET PATH

First published in hardback in Great Britain
by HarperCollins Publishers Ltd in 1994
First published in paperback by Picture Lions in 1995
This edition published by Collins Picture Books in 2003

1 3 5 7 9 10 8 6 4 2

ISBN-13: 978-0-00-782725-1

Picture Lions and Collins Picture Books are imprints of the Children's Division,
part of HarperCollins Publishers Ltd.

Text and illustrations copyright © Nick Butterworth 1994

The author/illustrator asserts the moral right to be identified
as the author/illustrator of the work.
A CIP catalogue record for this title is available
from the British Library.

Visit our website at: www.harpercollinschildrensbooks.co.uk

Printed in Malaysia

A TALE FROM PERCY'S PARK

THE SECRET PATH

NICK BUTTERWORTH

HarperCollins *Children's Books*

*I*n leafy green hedges,
   the doorway was wide.
You looked and you wondered
   and then stepped inside.
The puzzling pathways
   took you along,
A turn to the right
   turned out to be wrong.
But when all that seemed left
   turned out to be right,
You entered the centre,
   a wonderful sight!
But now comes the hard part,
   to find the right track,
To retrace your steps;
   the secret path back.
The maze is a trickster,
   of that there's no doubt.
The maze let you in,
   but it won't let you out!

"I know. It's a shame," said Percy the park keeper to his small friend.

Percy had been looking after a young squirrel who had fallen out of a tree and hurt his arm.

"And I bumped my nose on Thursday," went on the squirrel.

"Mmm, I see," said Percy, who was not really giving the squirrel his full attention.

Percy was busy searching for something.

"Aha! Here it is," said Percy. "String. We'll need this today."

As Percy and the squirrel trundled their way across the park, they didn't notice a group of friends hiding behind a large tree.

"I've been meaning to fix up the old maze for ages," said Percy. "The hedges are terribly overgrown."

"Percy's going to work on the maze," said the fox.

"Let's race him there and have some fun!" said the badger, and he began to whisper excitedly.

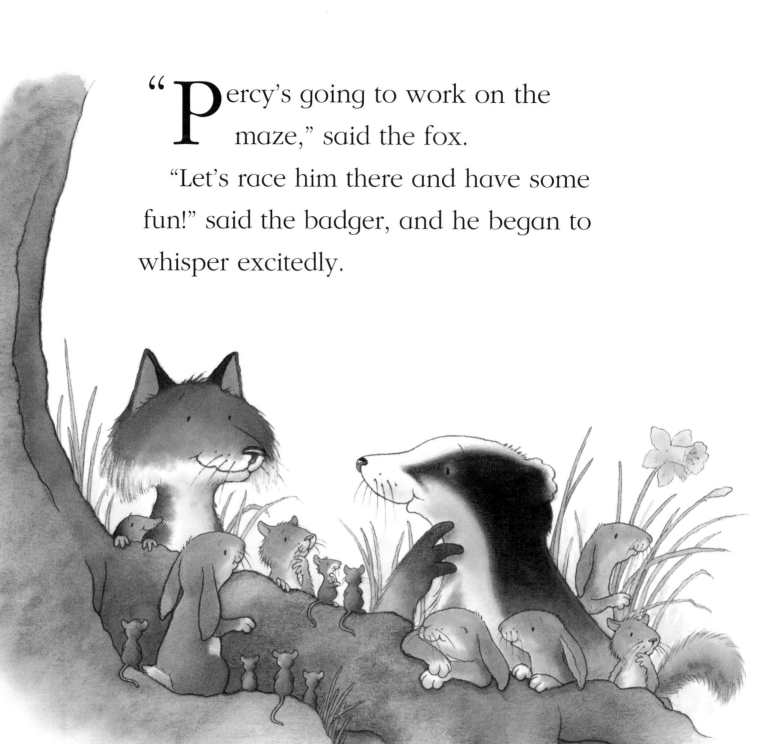

The others squeaked with delight as they listened. Only the hedgehog wasn't so sure. He found the maze rather confusing.

"I don't think I'll come," he said. "I've…er… got something to do."

P ercy parked his wheelbarrow by the entrance to the maze.

"Aren't you worried about getting lost in the maze?" the squirrel asked.

"That's why I need the string," said Percy. "I leave a trail of string from where I'm working back to the entrance of the maze. That way, I can't get lost, you see?"

The squirrel didn't really see because he wasn't really listening.

"I'm not sure if I like spring or autumn the best," he said.

At the back of the maze, a line of animals was disappearing one by one into the thick hedge.

"We'll go right to the middle and wait for Percy," whispered the badger.

"Then we'll jump out and give him a big surprise," giggled the rabbits.

"Ssshh!" said the fox loudly, which set them all giggling again.

ercy worked hard with his hedge clippers and little by little the maze began to look much tidier. All the time, Percy followed his string in and out of the maze.

By now, the surprise party had made its way
to the centre of the maze, where there stood
a stone bench. The bench had been carved to look
like a lion.

At first the animals waited eagerly for Percy to
come. But Percy took longer than they expected.
Soon they began to yawn. Then they fell asleep.

Percy's hedge clippers clacked on and on,
only stopping now and then when Percy
went to dump a barrow load
of clippings.

As Percy pushed his empty wheelbarrow back towards the maze, a hedgehog called to him.

"Hello Percy. Did you get a big surprise from the animals in the maze?"

"A big surprise?" Percy stopped and smiled. "Er…not yet," he said.

When at last Percy and the squirrel worked their way to the centre of the maze, there was no big surprise waiting for them.

Percy chuckled at the sight of the sleeping animals in front of him.

"Let's have some fun ourselves," he whispered.

Percy tiptoed to the back of the lion-shaped bench and coughed loudly.

"Ahem. I beg your pardon," said Percy in a deep, growly voice.

The fox opened one eye.

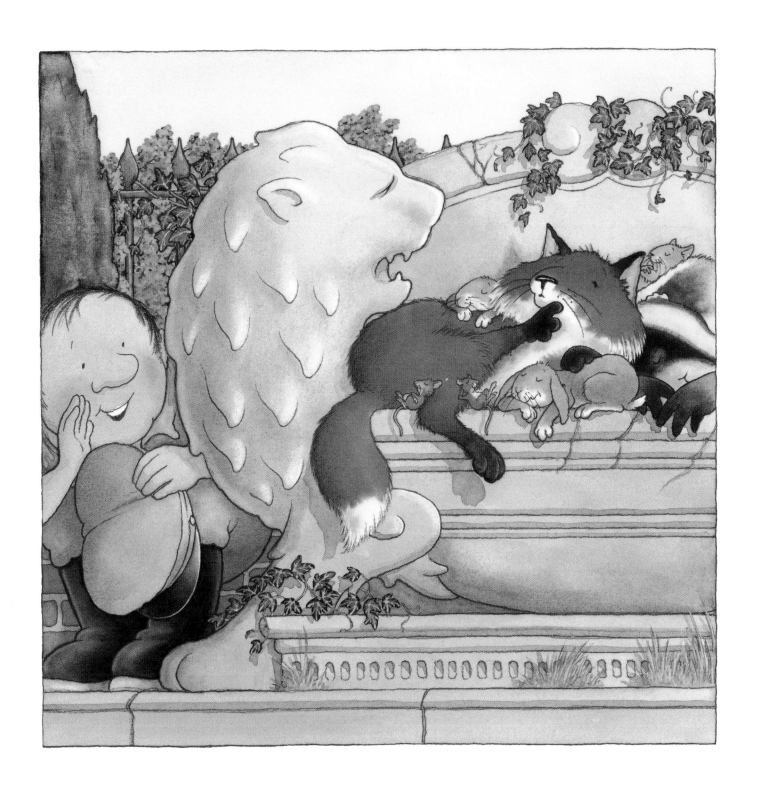

"It's not that I mind so very much," went on Percy, "but I do like people to ask before they go to sleep on me."

The other animals began to stir.

The fox stared at the lion's head.

He couldn't believe his ears.

"I'm very sorry," said the fox. "We didn't realise. We thought you were just a seat."
The other animals opened their eyes in amazement to hear the fox talking to a lump of stone. They were even more amazed when the stone answered back.

"Did you indeed?" said the growly voice.
"Just a seat.
Hmm."

"We're very sorry," said the fox. "Will you tell us your name?"

Percy growled. "My name is…"

But at that moment, one of the rabbits looked behind the bench.

"His name is Percy!" cried the rabbit.

The game was up and a chuckling Percy came out from behind the bench.

"Percy's tricked us, instead!" said the badger.

The fox suddenly started to giggle. That set everybody else giggling again.

"Come on," said Percy, as he collected his tools together, "who'd like toasted teacakes for tea? I'll show you the way out of the maze. All we have to do is to follow my str…"

ut Percy didn't finish. Standing there in front of him, was his little squirrel helper. The squirrel was holding a large ball of string.

"Don't forget this, Percy," he said. "I've wound it all up for you."

Percy looked dismayed.

"Don't worry," said the fox, "I think this is the way out."

"No, no," said the badger. "I'm sure it's this way."

"Surely it's this way," said another voice.

"I might be wrong," said the squirrel holding the ball of string, "but I've got a feeling it's this way."

Percy groaned.

"And I've got a feeling we'll be having toasted teacakes for breakfast!"

"I was born in London in 1946 and grew up in a sweet shop in Essex. For several years I worked as a graphic designer, but in 1980 I decided to concentrate on writing and illustrating books for children.

My wife, Annette, and I have two grown-up children, Ben and Amanda, and we have put down roots in Suffolk.

I haven't recently counted how many books there are with my name on the cover but Percy the Park Keeper accounts for a good many of them. I'm reliably informed that they have sold more than four million copies worldwide. Hooray!

I didn't realise this when I invented Percy, but I can now see that he's very like my mum's dad, my grandpa. Here's a picture of him giving a ride to my mum and my brother, Mike, in his old home-made wheelbarrow!"

Nick Butterworth has presented children's stories on television, worked on a strip for *Sunday Express Magazine* and worked for various major graphic design companies. Among his books published by HarperCollins are *Thud!, QPootle5* and *Jingle Bells*, but he is best-known for his stories about Percy the Park Keeper. There are now more than 30 books about Percy, who features on video, audio tape and CD, as well as having his own television series.

Percy the Park Keeper stories can be ordered at:
www.harpercollinschildrensbooks.co.uk